Ten Rowdy Ravens

Evon Zerbetz

Written by

Susan Ewing

Illustrated by

Evon Zerbetz

Ten rowdy ravens

Ready for a lark,

Nine race off while one remains

To holler "On your mark!"

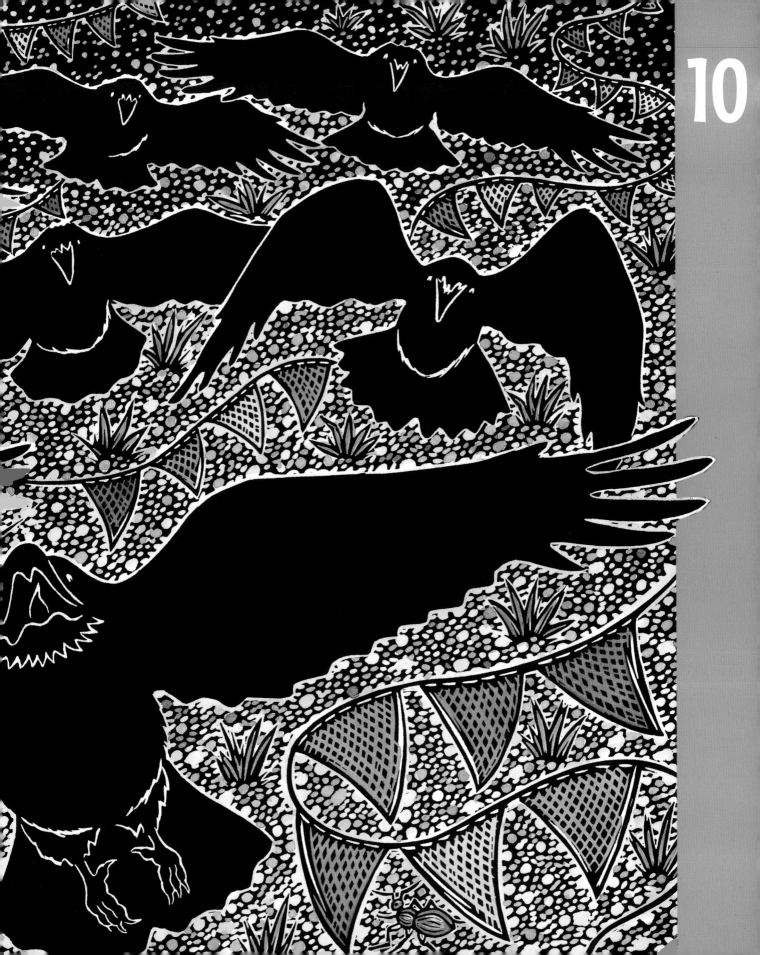

9

Nine raucous ravens
Tip a pail of bait,
Scramble in to pick a prize,
Twist of fate, now eight.

Eight roguish ravens

Pilfer piles of loot,

Cheater swipes some pretty pearls,

Seven give pursuit.

Seven reckless ravens
Play annoying tricks,
Pull a prank that pulls right back—
Oops! Only six.

Six rip-roaring ravens

Tuck, and roll, and dive,
After dizzy loop-de-loops,
The number left is five.

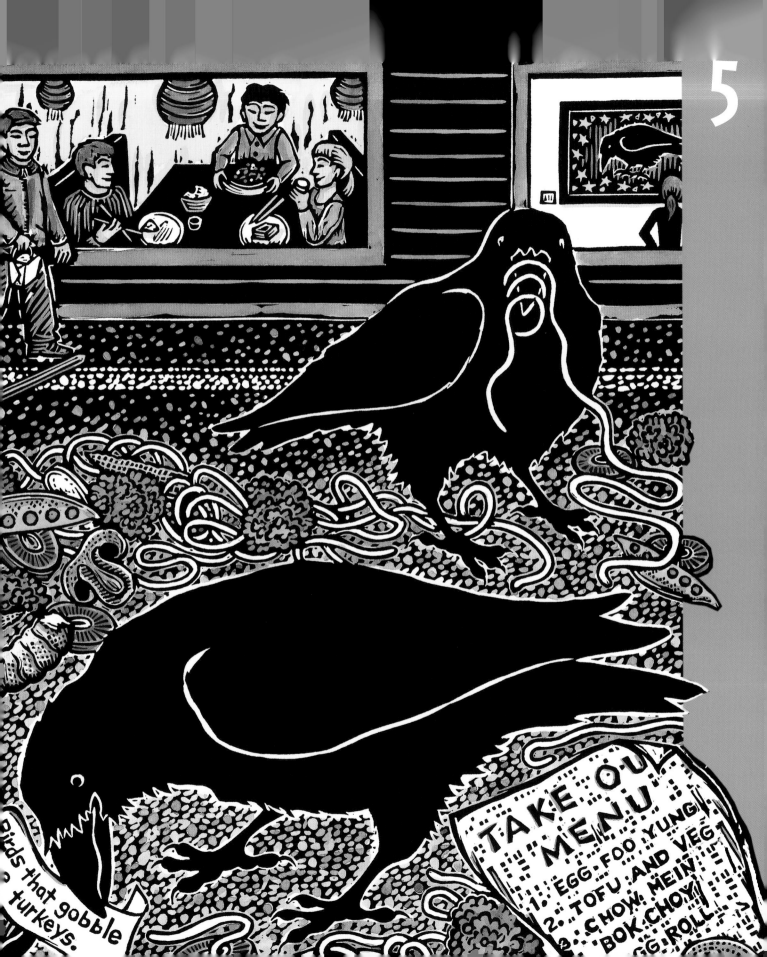

Four rakish ravens

Slide a slippery slope,

At the end one tumbles like

A bird-kaleidoscope.

Three crazy ravens

Hang out in the wind,
Flapping with the underwear—
Hanger-on gets pinned.

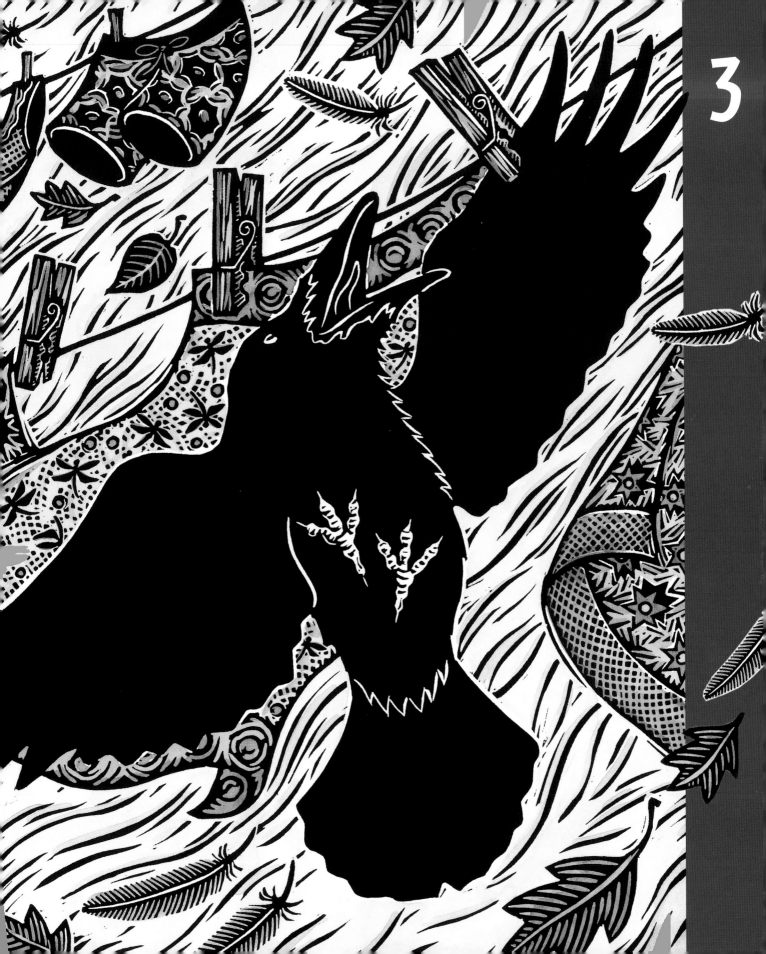

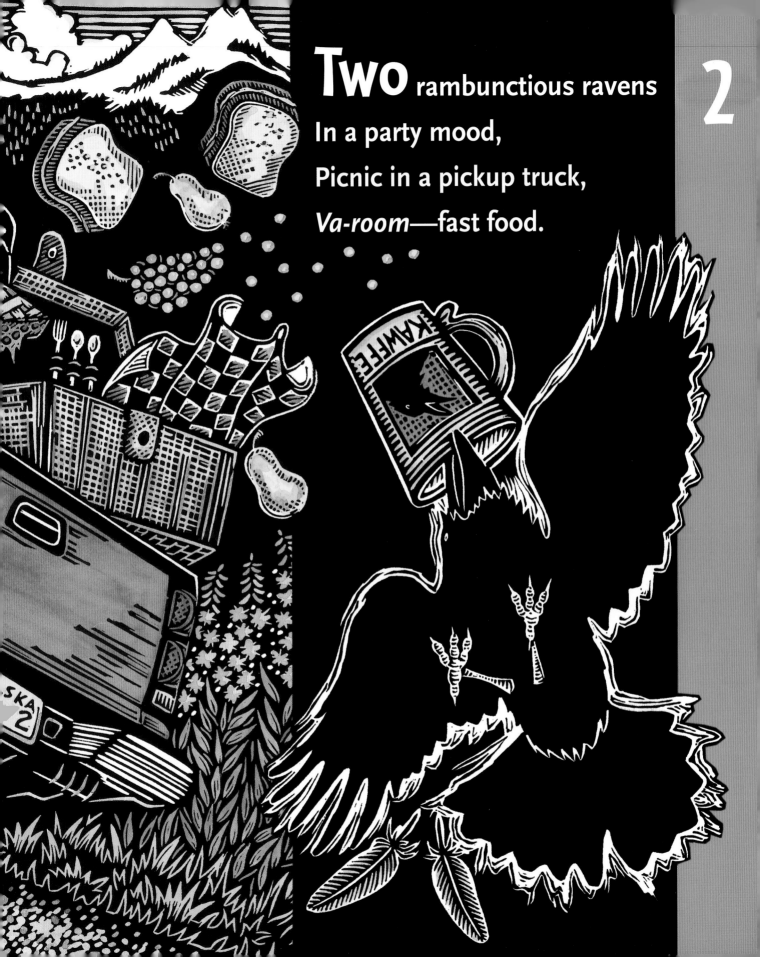

Two rambunctious ravens
In a party mood,
Picnic in a pickup truck,
Va-room—fast food.

2

KLA-WOCK!

One unruffled raven
Quickly counts to ten,
Kaws for all his friends to come
Begin the game again.

The Daily Kaw

25¢   TRUE NEWS FROM AROUND THE RAVEN WORLD   VOL. 1 NO. 10   7 PAGES

Clever Corvids Rule Bird World

Ravens, crows, magpies, and jays are all members of the Corvidae family of birds. Like all the corvid kin, ravens (*Corvus corax*) are extremely smart.

They range across the entire Northern Hemisphere and occupy almost every kind of habitat—from treeless arctic tundra, to hot desert, to dense forest, to open seashore, to countryside and town. Ravens are able to live in such a variety of places because they aren't picky about where they nest or what they eat. They build stick nests on cliffs, in trees, or on bridges or other structures, and will eat just about anything they can scavenge or hunt, including insects, grubs, seeds, fruit, fish, clams, mice, bird eggs, nestlings, carrion, leftover pizza, and cold chop suey.

Ravens are among the most playful of all animals. Young males are great showoffs, especially for females. They flip over rocks, drag around big sticks, crumple paper or leaves, and strut around with their feathers puffed out. Ravens pair up when they're about three years old and usually stay together all their lives.

It has been said that the smarter a creature is, the more mischief it can get into. Given the raven's intelligence and bold nature, it's no wonder that Raven the Trickster plays such an important role in folklore and myth. Stories are full of ravens who are sometimes good and sometimes bad—but always clever. Real life is also full of tales about daring, outrageous, funny, infuriating, and oh-so-smart ravens. Next time you spy some of these special characters, see if you can tell what they're up to— regular bird business or raven rabble-rousing.

Rowdy Ravens Ruin Easter Egg Hunt

JUNEAU, Alaska—Dozens of larcenous ravens stole 600 hard-boiled and plastic eggs that had been hidden in a large field for an Easter egg hunt. Minutes before the hunt, people noticed ravens flying by with colored eggs in their beaks. Rushing out to the field to check, volunteers found one, single egg remaining. Bits of bright-hued eggshell covered the ground like corvid confetti.

—Reported by Sherry Simpson in the Juneau Empire

Flying Fishers Cast Crumbs

GERMANY— A pair of clever ravens living near a resort hotel in the mountains observed that there were always leftover rolls in the hotel's garbage. It's no surprise that they stole the rolls, but these upper-crust corvids weren't satisfied with stale bread. Instead, they carried the rolls to their favorite perch above a nearby trout stream, and while one dropped bits of roll into the stream, the other took to the air and followed downstream, waiting for a fish to rise to the bait.

—Story shared by William DeArmond

California Corvids Catch Air

SANTA CRUZ ISLAND, Calif.— Rollicking ravens flock to California to surf the winds above rugged Santa Cruz Island. Their signature move is the "half-roll," where in mid-flight the bird tucks its wings and rolls onto its back, then rolls out again and continues flying. Observer Dirk Van Vuren saw one especially rompish raven perform an aerobatic sequence that included six half-rolls, two full rolls, and two double rolls.

—Reported in The Auk: Journal of the American Ornithologists' Union

Begging Bird Solves Doughnut Dilemma

ALASKA—An oil pipeline worker thought it would be amusing to frustrate a begging raven by tossing it two doughnuts—surely two chocolate-covered cakes

SEE PAGE 28

Translation: * Hey, let's go out for coffee!@ I'd love a mocha! Know of a good coffeehouse nearby?

Occasionally ravens can be seen drinking from pools of spilled coffee in a grocery store parking lot. Is it the cream? The coffee? or perhaps another ingredient that they like so much? What do you think?

Avian Aerialist Ousts Amateur

NEW MINAS, Nova Scotia—When Richard D. Elliot saw a raven hanging by its foot from a tree branch, he thought it was caught in something. But then the bird clamped onto the branch with its beak, let go with its foot, and hung there like a fancy black tassel. While the other ravens in the tree watched, the dexterous daredevil then gripped the branch with both feet and hung upside down like a bat. After repeating this performance, the avian aerialist flew up to perch on a higher branch.

A raven in the audience flew to the vacated branch and tried hanging by its beak, but had to flap its wings to keep from falling. The first raven came croaking down, drove the flapping bird from the branch, and demonstrated again how it was done. After the encore, all the birds flew away.

—*Reported in* The Auk: Journal of the American Ornithologists' Union

would be more than the persistent panhandler could carry. But the crafty raven put its beak through the hole of the first doughnut, clamped onto the second, and flew away with both.

—*From* Mind of the Raven, *by Bernd Heinrich*

Golfers Face Hijack Hazard

WRANGELL, Alaska—Golfers at the Muskeg Meadows Golf Course face a unique hazard. Rascally ravens pluck up golf balls while they're practically still rolling and carry them off to bury in the rough or drop around town. As a result, Wrangell golfers instituted Rule #8, the "Raven's Rule," which states, "A ball stolen by a raven may be replaced, with no penalty, provided there is a witness." Apparently other ravens don't count as witnesses.

—*Reported by Mary Lou Gerbi in* Alaskan Southeaster *magazine*

Pizza-packing Stashers Stuff Gutters

KETCHIKAN, Alaska—Greg and Harriet Zerbetz were eating soup by their kitchen window when they saw a raven with a slice of pizza in its beak land on the neighbor's roof. The raven stuffed the slice into the gutter, then ripped a swatch of moss off the shingles and covered the cached pizza with this cunning bit of camouflage. Harriet and Greg wondered if this was the same stasher who stuffed a bacon-greased paper towel in their own gutter, and bits of cookie and French fries under their shingles.

—*Story shared by Greg and Harriet Zerbetz*

Men on Maneuvers Hear *Haw Haw Haw*

ALEUTIAN ISLANDS, Alaska—In 1944, while assigned to the North Pacific Combat School, Charles Bradley and his men were on maneuvers, creeping through heavy fog along a ridgeline. They heard a mumble of voices in conversation, and then a burst of laughter. The fog thinned for a moment and the men saw what looked like a small group of people on a sloping patch of snow. One person was sliding down the snow on his backside while the others laughed uproariously. When the fog lifted again, the men were astonished to see five ravens calling *Haw! Haw! Haw!* as another bird slid down the slope. The frolicsome group kept at their game until the men could no longer contain their own belly laughs—at which the birds vanished.

—*From* Aleutian Echoes, *by Charles Bradley*

Super-size Takes Prize

JUNEAU, Alaska—Strolling through Brotherhood Park, Bob Armstrong noticed eight ravens standing in a circle. One after the other, each raven picked up an object—a shred of Styrofoam, wad of paper, whatever—and walked into the center of the circle to show off the souvenir. When one proud participant paraded into the ring with a giant soft drink cup, the other birds seemed to concede the game and all flew away.

—*Story shared by Bob Armstrong*

Stolen Steel Makes Novel Nest

PRUDHOE BAY, Alaska—A lack of trees in the far north didn't faze one resourceful raven pair—the love birds fashioned their nest out of interlaced welding rods stolen from a nearby construction site. Each steel "stick" was about a foot long and an inch and a half in diameter. Tucked onto the support girder of a large oil storage tank, the nest measured three feet high and four feet across. The industrious pair "feathered" their nest with such finishing touches as Teflon tape, work gloves, screwdrivers, and bright flagging tape.

—Story shared by Randy Scott

RAVEN GAMES

These two pictures might look the same, but are they? Can you find the 15 changes or missing things in the pictures below?

Be sure to find the 15 changes in these two pictures!

Neighborhood Underwear Plunder

PUGET SOUND, Wash. —One day Tony Angell heard his pet raven, Macaw, calling riotously, in a way that expressed the bird's frustration over trying to dislodge something. Tony whistled, and moments later Macaw appeared from the direction of the neighbor's with a clothespin in his beak. Tony traded some delicious overripe banana and chicken for the purloined clothespin.

The next morning, Tony heard the same racket, and soon spied the bird flying home with a white streamer. The rapturous raven landed and strutted to Tony, surely expecting something really terrific in trade for this prize pair of women's underwear clamped in his beak. Macaw had to stay inside on wash days for a while after that.

—From Ravens, Crows, Magpies and Jays, *by Tony Angell*

Tenth softbound printing 2018

Library of Congress Cataloging-in-Publication Data
Ewing, Susan, 1954-
    Ten rowdy ravens / by Susan Ewing ; illustrated by Evon Zerbetz.
       p. cm.
    ISBN-13 978-0-88240-606-0 (hardbound)
    ISBN-13 978-0-88240-610-7 (softbound)
    1. Counting—Juvenile literature. 2. Counting-out rhymes—Juvenile literature. I. Title: 10 rowdy ravens. II. Zerbetz, Evon, 1960- ill. III. Title.

    QA113.E877 2005
    513.2'11—dc22

                                                        2005014709

Alaska Northwest Books®
An imprint of

GRAPHIC ARTS
BOOKS®

GraphicArtsBooks.com

RAVEN READING LIST

Bird Brains, Candace Savage. Sierra Club Books, 1995.
Birds of Yellowstone, Terry McEneaney. Roberts Rinehart, 1988.
Crows: Encounters with the Wise Guys of the Avian World,
    Candace Savage. Douglas & McIntyre, 2005.
Guide to the Birds of Alaska, Robert H. Armstrong.
    Alaska Northwest Books, 2003.
In the Company of Crows and Ravens, Tony Angell and John Marzluff.
    Yale University Press, 2005.
Make Prayers to the Raven, Richard Nelson.
    University of Chicago Press, 1983.
Mind of the Raven, Bernd Heinrich.
    Ecco Press, an imprint of HarperCollins, 1999.
Ravens in Winter, Bernd Heinrich. Vintage Books,
    a division of Random House, 1989.
Ravens, Crows, Magpies and Jays, Tony Angell.
    University of Washington Press, 1978.

The pictures for this book are created from linoleum blocks that Evon carves, prints onto cotton paper, and hand colors. See more of Evon's whimsical artwork and learn about the process of creating her imagery at www.evonzerbetz.com.

Editor: Michelle McCann
Designer: Elizabeth Watson

Printed in China

In memory of my beloved malamute Chena, who the ravens pegged as somebody special from the very beginning.

—S. E.

A Ten Kaw salute to pals Kim and Sara, and to Sue, who always peeks at the progress in my studio before yoga.

—E. Z.

CORVID CLASSIFIEDS

SBFR Looking for SBMR for flying and hunting activities. Call KRRR-KRWWAH

For Rent: 3-bedroom nest located in good neighborhood near pizza house and burger joint.

Cache and Carry Sale
Everything must go. Sa[...] Wolf Lane.
Early birds pay do[...]

Exten[...]

Tru[...]
aft[...]

Roo[...]
Meet [...] dish
to share. [...] Cabin
Grocery.

Kah-m[...]ty Kalend[...]

MOVIES
The Raven (P[...]sho[...]

MUSIC
Rave D[...]
St[...]

[...]olor of eye, **2.** missing fork, **3.** number on card [...] dot to blue, **5.** flipped the pear, [...] front, **8.** "stop"

CORVID CLASSIFIEDS

ESTATE SALE
Extensive collection of shiny things. Preview at noon, auction begins at 1 P.M. Crow-tary Beach

TRUCK FOR SALE – CORVUS MODEL RAVE-XT
Low mileage, good condition, make offer. KAH... after 10.

LOST:
Gold Locket. Sentimental valu...

LOST:
1962 World's Fair Spa... Pine Lake picnic ar... KRR-ROOK

RO...
...nd friends. Bring... ...m. at the dumpste... ...Log...

NEST REPAIR...
No job too small or to... Will trade work for p...to...s.
Call KAH-KALK...

FRESH HALIBUT F/V CORVID Bar Harbor ramp 8.

NEST BUILDERS
Just in, fresh wolf fur for nest lining. Call WOL-FYIP

CORVID CLASSIFIEDS

ART EX...
"...von Zerbetz's linocuts from ...night with a

..."Raven's Tail Weaving" M... ...al raven community hall.

...loor Events

...T TO ROOST RUNNIN...
...sored by the Raven R... ...Ma...p... Marshes.

...WATCHERS HIKE
...ay ...M. Me...at Bird Be... Bring bi...cul...rs.

GO FLY...KIT...
Annual e...ent s...on... 2–3 P.M. School s...

Reci...

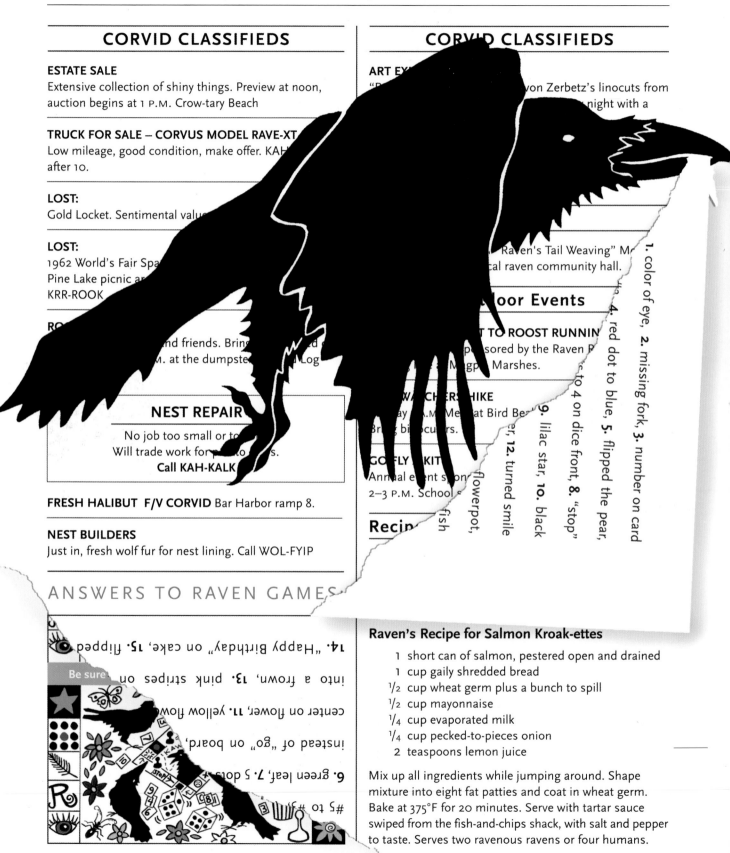

ANSWERS TO RAVEN GAMES

1. color of eye, 2. missing fork, 3. number on card, 4. red dot to blue, 5. flipped the pear, 6. green leaf, 7. 5 dots ...#5 to #3, 8. "stop", 9. lilac star, 10. black, 11. yellow flower center on flower, 12. turned smile ...fish ...flowerpot, 13. pink stripes on ...instead of "go" on board, 14. "Happy Birthday" on cake, 15. flipped ...into a frown,

Be sure...

Raven's Recipe for Salmon Kroak-ettes

- 1 short can of salmon, pestered open and drained
- 1 cup gaily shredded bread
- ½ cup wheat germ plus a bunch to spill
- ½ cup mayonnaise
- ¼ cup evaporated milk
- ¼ cup pecked-to-pieces onion
- 2 teaspoons lemon juice

Mix up all ingredients while jumping around. Shape mixture into eight fat patties and coat in wheat germ. Bake at 375°F for 20 minutes. Serve with tartar sauce swiped from the fish-and-chips shack, with salt and pepper to taste. Serves two ravenous ravens or four humans.